The Cabbage Moth
AND THE
Shamrock

A STORY BY Ethel Marbach
ILLUSTRATED BY Michael Hague

Green Tiger Press

PUBLISHED BY SIMON & SCHUSTER

NEW YORK · LONDON · TORONTO · SYDNEY · TOKYO · SINGAPORE

GREEN TIGER PRESS

Simon & Schuster Building, Rockefeller Center

1230 Avenue of the Americas, New York, New York 10020

GREEN TIGER PRESS is an imprint of Simon & Schuster.

Designed by Marc Cheshire

Manufactured in the United States of America

5 7 9 10 8 6 4

Library of Congress Cataloging-in-Publication Data

Pochocki, Ethel, 1925-

The cabbage moth and the shamrock / by Ethel Marbach ;

illustrated by Michael Hague.

p.   cm.

Summary: Separated after a summer spent enjoying each other's

company, a cabbage moth and a shamrock are reunited

by an old lady who appreciates their beauty.

[1. Moths—Fiction. 2. Plants—Fiction.]

I. Hague, Michael, ill. II. Title.

PZ7.P7495Cab   1991

[E]—dc20   91-575

ISBN 0-671-74864-5

here was once a cabbage moth named Fiona who was sadly plain and dull-looking. She was not beautiful, as one might expect a Fiona to be, with large wings swirled in orange and yellow, with black stripes and dots of white, nor did she cause people to catch their breath in delight to watch her flutter by, up and up into a blue August sky.

Rather, she was very small and pale, with not a whit of color to turn an eye. She looked as if she had spent her life in the shade. The only attention she received came in sudden sharp voices of exasperation from ladies tending their gardens.

"Drat that moth! Watch it, there she goes! Quick, kill her before she gets to the cabbages!"

Fiona got to know that tone and would head immediately for the low-lying white briar roses in the field, where she would stop quivering and lay flat on the petals and try to get hold of herself. She would stay there while the ladies sought out snails and squash bugs and other enemies and finally went inside to check their blueberry pies in the oven.

Fiona was timid as well as plain. If she had fingernails, she would have chewed them. And she had no talents to speak of.

She could not spin a web and catch the morning dew in a rainbow. She could not rub her legs together and make music as the crickets did in the fall or sing a treesong as the spring peepers did, or light up the sky in a sprinkle of fireworks as

fireflies did on a June evening, nor could
she make honey from wildflowers as her
friends the bees did.

What she did mostly was chew holes in cabbages, not because she was a bad moth but because it was her nature to chew holes in cabbages. When she was not doing this, she sat by herself and thought a lot. She had few friends and most of these were other undesirables whose aim in life was to eat, hide, and not get caught.

Maeve, the green broccoli worm, had a sour disposition because of her nervous stomach. She never knew when the bud she lived in would be picked and she would be thrown into an icy brine to curl up and die; or, if she escaped the briny bath, be boiled and served with butter on the broccoli. Conrad the Snail and

Drusilla the Cornborer were passing ac-
quaintances who lived in different worlds,
but at least they greeted her civilly and did
not turn away from her with a wrinkled
nose.

Fiona yearned with all her heart to be a
breathtaking creature, for underneath her
quiet drab surface, she was a real Fiona, a
dazzling, fiery queen, a monarch who
rippled the air with sweet wafts of honey-
suckle and wild cranberry blossoms. (The
outside Fiona always smelled faintly of
sauerkraut.) The inside Fiona sought out
beauty wherever she was. She explored the
shell of a periwinkle and listened to the
echo of her soft hello. She sat for an hour

on the sleeve of a red velvet dress hung out for a spring airing, sinking into its deep lush redness with joy. She hovered about a little girl who had come into the garden to play her flute for the fairies and danced and danced as the notes hit the sky like crystals.

She wanted so very much to add to the world's beauty, to be brilliant, to be admired. She thought wistfully that she would even wish to be loved. But although she might be shy and plain and a dreamer, she was not dumb. She knew the

facts and she accepted them. So she worked at being contented with what she had, a hard enough job, and she held onto her name to keep her heart light in dark times. Oh, how she loved her name! Just suppose it had been Bertha, or Hermione, or Mildred, or Soggybottom. The very thought of it made her count her blessings.

She did have one friend outside the bug world who was very dear to her and his name was Jeremy. He was a shamrock, one of a bunch living under the purple apple tree. She had met him one hot July afternoon when she was being chased by an angry lady with a fly swatter.

She was flying in wild, fearful circles when he snapped, "Down here, quick! Under the bramble leaf!"

He had saved her life, for the leaf was so large it draped itself over the shivering white wings, and the lady stormed away, unable to find that pesky thing. Fiona thanked Jeremy and they told each other their names. They agreed that they were exceptionally lovely and suited each other perfectly.

"Fiona . . . it is delicate and graceful and airy. It is a small white fairy with red hair and a gypsy wit," said Jeremy.

"Jeremy . . . one with such a name is gentle and brave, a gentleman and a scholar, kingly but humble," said Fiona.

"I like a butterfly that isn't bold or gaudy, always showing off as if she owned the world and clashing with the colors of flowers. Oh, how that hurts my eyes!" said Jeremy. "You are pure as the first snow and no matter what flower you touch, you add to its brilliance, like a poppy or scarlet snapdragon, or you bring out its softness, like a daffodil or larkspur." Fiona did not

tell him that she was not a true butterfly and that she lived among coarse cabbage leaves. She loved him too deeply to take away his illusions.

"I love your green. It is so alive and full of hope and cheer, no matter what. You're sure of yourself without being arrogant. You have the manners of a prince and the simplicity of one close to the earth," said Fiona, happily adding up his virtues.

And so they spent the summer of contented days and nights in each other's company. They shared the sweet smell of wheat cut to hay and the music of quiet winds ruffling the aspens. They survived

the constant dangers of predatory humans, greedy birds, heavy rains, drought, small children with heavy feet and butterfly nets and scythes. By late September, when the mellow chants of the crickets had replaced the happy questions of the May peepers and the August katydids, Jeremy's green had faded and was tinged with spots of brown. He did not stand as princely tall as when Fiona first found her true love.

And Fiona's wings fluttered more slowly each day. She shivered now more with the fall chill than with delight over the trill of a flute. They knew that changes would be coming to their life soon but they would not think of them now, this minute. They would continue to delight in the fact that by God's good grace, they had found each other at all.

One day a high blustery wind carried Fiona away from Jeremy over the tops of goldenrod and purple asters, onto a tuft of sailing milkweed down. It whirled the moth and down through spirals of sky and then suddenly, sharply, to earth, onto a clump of oak leaves already dried out and crinkly by the side of the road. Fiona lay still and unmoving on her puff down.

She was dead. The silky strands of milkweed enveloped her in the shimmery pale
beauty of a royal princess asleep.

Before she could be squashed by a boy
riding down the road on a bike, or a horse,
or a dog chasing a squirrel, Fiona was
found by an old lady. She had been limp-
ing along the road, her eyes squinting and
searching for whatever might please her.
When she came to Fiona, she stopped and
smiled and a hundred wrinkles made
roadways on her face. She picked up
Fiona and her bed of down and laid her
gently in the basket over her arm. She
passed through the plumes of goldenrod

and hobbled through the grass gingerly, as if in pain. She paused by the gnarled apple tree still heavy with small purple apples, rummaged below it and picked two apples and a handful of peppermint sprigs. Then she came to the clump of shamrocks, bent down, picked Jeremy, and laid him in the basket next to Fiona.

She made her way back to the road and followed its curve, stopping now and then to ease her pain, and to pick a few hazelnuts for the pocket of her brown sweater, or look up at the geese honking their way across the sky.

She came soon to a small red house with a black and white cat named Max sitting on the step. Max rubbed against her legs and wound his tail in and out of

them. She put her basket down on a wooden table inside the house and poured Max some milk from a can into a chipped blue bowl. Then she emptied the contents of her basket onto the table and peace came over her face and excitement into her eyes.

She went over to a box labelled SCRAPS—FEED BAGS and took out a small rough piece of burlap. She brought it to the table, along with scissors, a pot of paste, crayons, and a cigar box of odds and ends. She began to cut and paste and snip and draw, until the sun which had shone brightly through her little window when she began grew dim and the reflection of the setting sun glowed warm and pink on the pane.

At last she stopped, rubbed her eyes, and put her hands in her lap. Max jumped up on the table and purred, "Yes, yes, that is very nice, my dear mistress, now would you have a bit of liver sausage for me, perhaps?" She lifted the burlap so he might not hurt it with his jumping and tacked it onto the wall with two rusty thumbtacks.

She fed Max one half of a cold sausage and ate the other half herself, took the two apples and the handful of hazlenuts out of her pocket and put them on the table. Then she unwrapped a hard heel of pumpernickel bread from its brown wrapper and made a cup of peppermint tea.

She sighed with contentment . . . how rich were today's gifts! . . . and admired her handiwork on the wall.

On the burlap she had drawn with green crayon a border of ivy leaves, attaching Jeremy at the bottom with Fiona poised directly above him, as if ready to alight. Above them she had printed:

LIVE IN THE JOYOUS
MIRACLE OF NOW!

Under the protecting arch of NOW!,
Fiona and Jeremy had been reunited
and would live forever, as all true lovers
do. They showed that everything God
has made can give a joy unable to be
measured. Even a cabbage moth and a
shamrock.